Book 10

Sara and the Secret Mission

The Ituria Chronicles

J.B. MOONSTAR

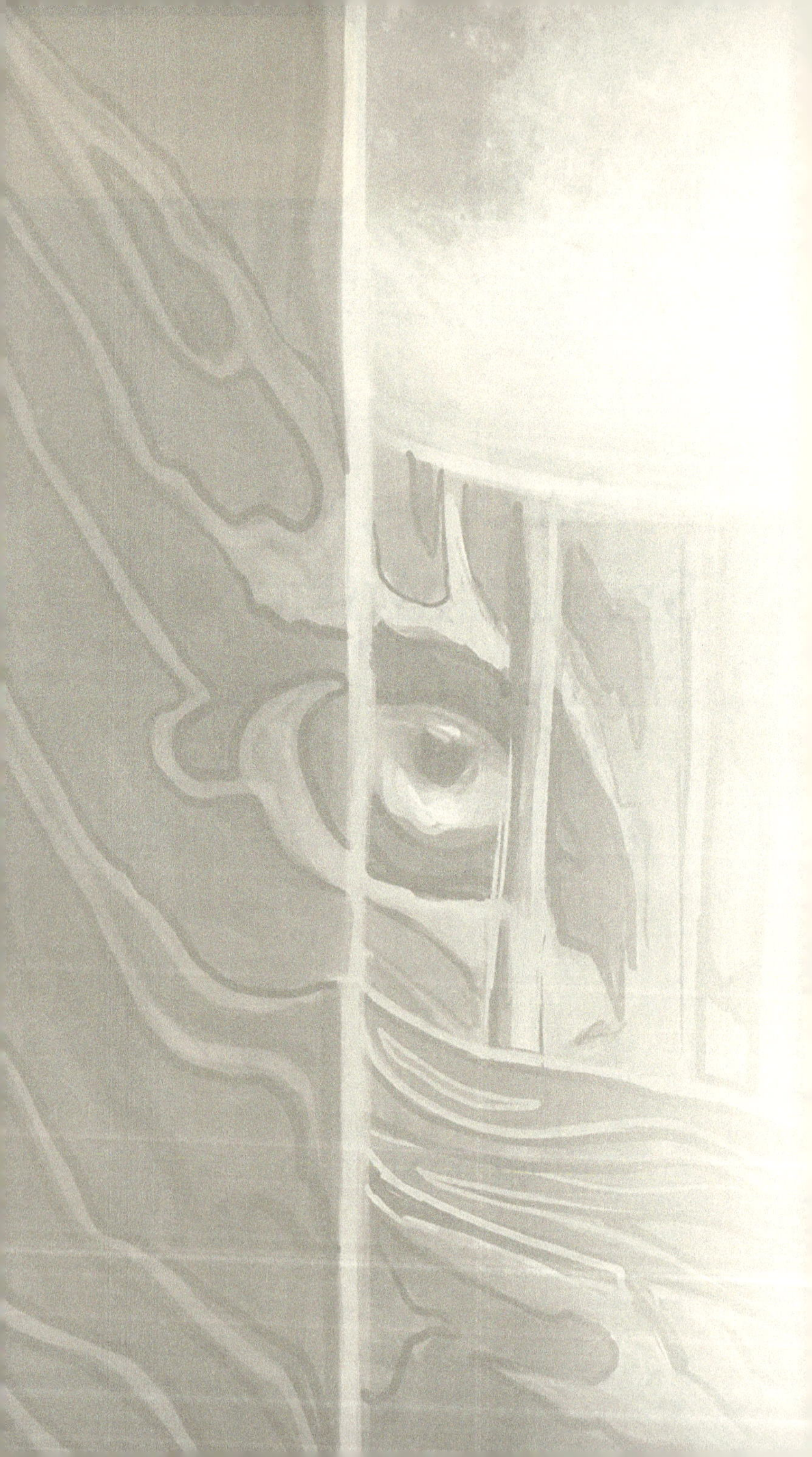

Sara and the Secret Mission

The Ituria Chronicles

J.B. Moonstar

Published By: The Little Horsemen an imprint of 4 Horsemen Publications, Inc.

The Little Horsemen Publications
℅ 4 Horsemen Publications, Inc.
PO Box 419
Sylva, NC 28779
4horsemenpublications.com
info@4horsemenpublications.com

Cover &Illustration by Jenn Kotick. Contact for commssions at Jkotickart@gmail.com .

Typesetting by Niki Tantillo

Editor CI Stearns

Library of Congress Control Number: 2022949004

Paperback ISBN-13: 979-8-8232-0135-3
Hardcover ISBN-13: 979-8-8232-0136-0
Audiobook ISBN-13: 979-8-8232-0133-9
Ebook ISBN-13: 979-8-8232-0134-6

DEDICATION

To the National Geographic Researcher/Explorer Allison Skidmore, and National Geographic Writer Dina Fine Maron, for their bravery in reporting the story of Amur Tigers and their fight for survival. Thank you for your courage, in the face of adversity, to bring the truth about illegal hunting of Amur Tigers to the world!

Dear Reader,

In my continuing chronicles of Ituria's Alliance, I am relaying a story that started as a cry for help that wakes Sara, a young girl living in a small town in the countryside. The continuing calls compel Sara to slip out of her home to find the source. She doesn't realize it was not a call she heard with her ears, but with her mind—a mother tiger is calling out for help to save her cubs!

But to save them, Sara must first find the cubs, and then hide them away from the poachers seeking to trap them. She must rely on her wits and courage to see it through; there is no turning back once she starts on her mission. Can she rescue the baby tigers, get them to safety, and get back home without anyone noticing she is gone? Can she stay one step ahead of the poachers?

Sincerely,

Knocker,

First Guard to Ituria

Table of Contents

CHAPTER ONE
Voice in the Night 1

CHAPTER TWO
Tiger Eyes 6

CHAPTER THREE
Race to the Den 11

CHAPTER FOUR
Distraction 15

CHAPTER FIVE
Lost in the Woods 20

CHAPTER SIX
A Second Attack 25

CHAPTER SEVEN
An Unexpected Journey 29

CHAPTER EIGHT
Meeting Ituria 34

CHAPTER NINE
Angela Introduces Herself 39

CHAPTER TEN
Returning Home 43

CHAPTER ELEVEN
Late Night Discussion 48

CHAPTER TWELVE
Making a Plan 52

CHAPTER THIRTEEN
    RESCUING THE CUBS 57
CHAPTER FOURTEEN
    TRICKING THE POACHERS 62
CHAPTER FIFTEEN
    ANOTHER PATH. 68
CHAPTER SIXTEEN
    CONFRONTATION 73
CHAPTER SEVENTEEN
    RACE FOR HOME. 78
CHAPTER EIGHTEEN
    NEW MEMBER OF THE ALLIANCE 83

NOTE FROM THE AUTHOR 88
BOOK CLUB QUESTIONS 90
ABOUT THE AUTHOR 91

Chapter One

VOICE IN THE NIGHT

Sara could stay still no longer. She slipped out of the house and ran through the moonlit yard, heading in the direction of the forest. The voice she heard was frantic—*her children were in danger, and she couldn't get to them!* Following an abandoned logging road, she ran to the forest edge. The trees here were all new growth trees, the trunks slender and tall; most of the old trees were cut down on the orders of the logging company years ago. Soft moonlight allowed her to see the dirt road, but it did not provide enough light through the leaves to see what might lie in the forest beyond.

She stopped before entering the forest, trying to determine the direction of the voice. Should she go further down or was this the right place? She couldn't tell anymore! The sound of running footsteps on the road heading in her direction grabbed her attention, and she slipped quickly into the darkness of the nearest group of trees hoping she hadn't been seen.

Local officials were extremely strict about the commoners being out at night—it was not allowed! They claimed it was for the protection of the people; however, Sara knew it was to let the poachers roam free in the forest at night, hunting whatever they could kill under cover of darkness.

Waiting until she no longer heard the footsteps, she turned her focus back to the voice. It was still calling to her, and she listened carefully to the words she heard.

"Please rescue my babies! I cannot get to them; they need someone to help them, or they will die!" The voice was desperate; however, Sara realized it was not loud. It sounded more like an echo—surrounding Sara, swirling around her; she could not put a direction on where it was coming from. She turned anxiously in one direction, then the next—she didn't know which way to go!

Suddenly, a boy appeared beside her; someone she had never seen before. He was tall, but looked only a few years older than her, 14 years old or so. In the dark, she could see he held a large bag with a strap over his shoulder. It was hard to see much else, but as his eyes caught the moonlight, they were bright green, almost glowing!

"What are you doing out?" he whispered urgently. "You know the rules!"

"Did you hear it too?" she whispered back with equal urgency. "I heard a call for help, a mother is searching for her children to rescue them, but she can't get to them! I must help her!"

"You shouldn't be out here; they will find you!" the boy replied, looking quickly down the road in both directions, then back at her. "You can't be out here tonight!"

"What are you doing out here then?" Sara asked defiantly.

"I heard gunshots, and then a loud cry—someone calling for help!" the boy said. "What did you hear?"

Sara paused for a moment, and then softly and slowly spoke the words she was still hearing all around her. "Please rescue my babies! I cannot get to them; they need help, or they will die!" There was no longer an urgency in the voice, now only a deep sadness.

"Can't you hear her?" Sara asked him, wondering why she could still hear it if he could not.

"Where is it coming from?" the boy asked, watching Sara's face in the moonlight. Her face looked frightened, her eyes wide as she looked fearfully around her, looking past his face to make sure there was no one on the road. Yet he could hear the determination in her voice; she needed to help whoever was calling to her.

"That's the problem!" she whispered frantically. "I can't tell any longer, it's surrounding me, everywhere and nowhere at the same time!" She turned and looked back into his eyes, searching for something to confirm he was hearing it too.

"Is it the voice of someone you know in the area?" he asked quietly. "Do you recognize who it could be?"

"No, I don't know who it is, just a voice calling to me. Do you hear it? Or is it only me? I don't understand!" Sara's voice got louder as she started to panic.

"Shhhh … keep your voice down!" he said quietly, trying to keep her calm. "We will figure it out. I believe you because I heard something earlier … but I don't hear anything now." He paused for a few seconds, then continued as he put his hands on her shoulders, his green eyes looking directly into her eyes. "You can still hear it, right?"

"Yes, I do, a mother calling for someone to help her children!" Sara replied, looking into his eyes, searching for a logical explanation. Without thinking, she reached up and grasped the necklace her father gave her several weeks ago. She had come to use it as a calming spirit in her crazy world. When she held it in her hand, it gave her the sense that things would be okay.

"What are you holding in your hand?" the boy asked as he noticed her actions.

His question put her back into panic mode, and she immediately let go of the necklace, quickly hiding it underneath her sweater. She remembered her father's dire warning to her when he gave it to her, "Don't let anyone know you have this! Keep it hidden and it will protect you!" She understood the warning, it was a tiger's claw he found when cutting logs, illegal to own unless you were a poacher who would sell it and split the money with the border guards.

"It's nothing … a gift from my father," she said in a strained tone. "Nothing to worry about."

But the boy continued with his questions, "Maybe this necklace is the reason you can still hear the voice … it is possible." He was silent for a few moments, thinking to himself. Then he asked softly, "Can I see the necklace?"

Chapter Two

TIGER EYES

"What do you mean?" Sara asked anxiously. "It's just a necklace, nothing more, just a family thing."

"No, it is more, I can tell," he said softly, intrigued by what he had seen when she held the necklace in her hand. "It does something to your eyes when you hold it, don't you feel it?"

Sara backed up quickly and the boy's hands slipped from her shoulders. She didn't like where this was going. Yes, it was true, she was aware holding the claw changed her emotionally, she could feel it helping her to calm down, but what was he talking about, what did he see?

"I have to get home!" she said nervously as she turned away.

"No, wait!" he replied, gently calling her back. "I mean you no harm, please believe me! And I won't be turning you in if the necklace is something you think you shouldn't have, okay?"

Sara looked back at him, then clasped the necklace in her fingers again. The calm feeling returned, and she could hear a soft voice talking to her in her mind. "It's okay, you can trust this one."

"It happened again," the boy said softly. "Whatever that necklace is, when you hold it, your eyes change color, from deep brown to glowing gold, almost like tiger eyes." The complete calmness in his voice as he revealed what he saw caught Sara off guard.

"What are you talking about?" she replied sharply, trying to contain her uneasiness at this conversation. "That's just the moonlight when it shines in my eyes. Nothing to do with my necklace!"

"Okay, let's just start over again. Hello, my name is Marcus, but my friends call me Knocker, a nickname I acquired years ago when I was younger. What is your name?" the boy asked in a friendly voice, wanting to show he meant her no harm.

"Hello Knocker, my name is Sara," she replied nervously.

"Sara, while many humans are not aware of it, some items can help you communicate with animals, and your necklace may be one of those items." Knocker was talking calmly and softly, looking at her with his bright green eyes.

"But that is not our current problem," he continued as his voice became serious. "You can hear a voice calling out, but I can't. Do you agree?"

Sara nodded her head, but she didn't answer further.

"The voice must be flowing through the necklace to you, that is why you can't place which direction it is in," he continued. "It is all around you, the necklace can hear it and it's relaying the calls to you … do you still hear the voice?"

Standing perfectly still and closing her eyes, Sara could hear the voice of the mother, calling for someone to help her children. It was like an echo, flowing around her and encircling her, coming from everywhere and nowhere.

"Yes, I do," she responded quietly as she opened her eyes again. Now calmer and even more determined, she continued, "Let's help the mom and her babies, and then we can deal with your questions about the necklace, okay?"

"That would be my suggestion, too," Knocker said as he once again glanced up and down the dirt road. "Close your eyes and ask the voice where she is and where her children are."

Nodding to Knocker, Sara asked in a hushed whisper, "Where are you, where are your children? How can I help you?" Then she listened for an answer. The voice she heard got louder as it swirled and echoed around her. Emotions swept over her as she could feel the anguish of this mother, trying to save her children. The voice was reaching into her consciousness to form the answer. Sara repeated the words to Knocker as she heard them herself, the voice was answering through her.

"Please save my children, I can no longer get to them," was the reply, echoing through her head as she spoke the words aloud.

"Where are you?" Knocker asked quietly.

"I was chased away from my den by humans," it replied through Sara softly and slowly, sadness in every word. "I was hit, and I am no longer able to move. There is no hope for me, you must save my children."

Sara gasped, awakening from the trance—the emotions were too strong to bear. Whoever or whatever this mother was, she was viciously chased and attacked by the poachers that prowled the woods at night.

"What else did she say?" Knocker asked softly, hoping to get Sara to focus again, they needed more information.

"She says there is no hope for her," Sara relayed to him slowly, repeating the words she heard; then added fervently, "We must give her peace—we must find and save her children!"

"Ask where her children are, a way we can find them!" Knocker whispered back.

"Where is your den? Where are your children, how can we find them?" Sara repeated and waited for a response. The voice answered her, and she relayed the information to Knocker.

"Her den is on a hill just past the turn in the road to the north. We will know it by the lone tree standing in front of it. All the other trees were taken." Sara said as she looked to the north and the curve in the road. "That's the way we need to go!"

But as she uttered the words and pointed to the north, a vehicle came around the curve in the road heading south, headlights blazing, speeding down the road. The sound of men shouting could be heard, even over the engine of the vehicle.

Sara turned to Knocker and whispered, "Hurry, we have to beat them to the children!"

Chapter Three

RACE TO THE DEN

The vehicle drove down the road for several hundred yards, then the driver slammed on the brakes, driving it off to the side of the road and bringing the vehicle to a screeching halt. Three men got out and quickly headed into the forest on the west side of the road, shouting as they ran. Flashlights shined through the tree trunks as they searched for the mother they had shot.

"This way!" shouted one. "I've found some paw prints!"

"Great, Tony! Let's grab the mother first, then we can go back and get the cubs!" another shouted as he headed south, following the first into the forest.

Watching from behind the trees across the road, Knocker and Sara nodded to each other and silently started working their way north. They needed to get past these men to get to the den before the men had time to backtrack and find the cubs. The men's yelling and noisy trampling through the trees to the west of the road allowed Knocker and Sara to quietly pass them on the east side. Approaching the curve in the road, Knocker could see a lone tall tree in front of a small cave on the side of a hill. Small saplings surrounded it, but the lone mature tree towered above them.

Pointing it out to Sara, he whispered, "That must be her den!"

Nodding, Sara added quietly, "We will have to cross the road. Let's go a little further north, so that the trees on this side will block us from their view when we cross."

Knocker nodded in agreement, and they went north of the den before crossing the road.

As they reached the other side, Sara heard a new voice but just as urgent. "They have found her; you must hurry to save the cubs!"

"Knocker," Sara whispered, "the voice says they have found the mother, we must hurry!"

"We're not far now, let's go!" Knocker replied, running through the smaller trees with Sara following close behind.

The sound of yelling in the distance revealed that the poachers were dragging the mother tiger's body to the vehicle. Once they reached the truck and she was loaded into the back, they would be off to catch the cubs!

As they approached the den, Knocker called softly inside, "Hey little ones, your mother has sent us to help you, please come out quickly!"

Sara wondered why Knocker thought the cubs would understand him. However, watching with amazement, she saw three little tiger cubs, just barely able to walk, waddling to the front of the den and peeking out cautiously. Knocker knelt beside them, speaking quietly, "We are here to help you. Your mom can't make it back now, and she sent us to rescue you."

Sara watched in silence as this boy was able to communicate with these little cubs, she was not sure how; but now was not the time for reason—*my necklace is talking to me, why shouldn't Knocker be able to talk to animals?* She would accept the unexplained for now and look for answers tomorrow. Tonight, anything that helps them rescue the cubs is appreciated!

The little cubs looked sad and confused, their eyes wide and looking around for their mom, wondering what was happening.

"Let me carry you in my bag, as we need to leave the area as soon as possible, okay?" he asked.

The tiger cubs walked over to Knocker and allowed him to pick them up and put them in the bag. As he put the third one in the bag, the voice returned to Sara. "They are too close now, you can't run to escape, you must hide!"

"Knocker," Sara whispered, "they are almost here. The voice says to hide, we won't be able to escape. What can we do?"

"Listen," Knocker answered quickly as he put the bag with the cubs in her hands. "You and the cubs must go back into the den, go to the far back and hide. If you talk to the cubs softly, they will understand you, okay? Tell them to keep quiet, as quiet as they can."

"What?" Sara exclaimed in disbelief, knowing she couldn't talk to them, even if Knocker could.

"I'll explain later, no time now!" Knocker whispered urgently. "I will lead the poachers away, but you must be hidden, so they only see me, okay? Once I lead them away, you and the cubs need to go into the forest and find another place to hide. I will find you! Now go quickly!"

There was no time to discuss options! Sara clutched the bag close to her as she ducked inside of the den and crawled to the back. The den curved a little bit in the back, so she went to where she couldn't see the opening, that meant they couldn't see her either!

"Listen little ones," she said softly, hoping Knocker was right and they would understand. "It is important that we stay here and be very quiet!"

"Okay," came a small voice from the bag, "we will be quiet. Please don't leave us alone!"

"I will stay with you," Sara whispered as she held the bag close. "I will keep you safe!"

Outside the den, the shouting was getting closer.

"This way, guys!" one yelled. "I can see the tracks, follow me!"

Chapter Four

DISTRACTION

"Wait up, Doug!" shouted another. "Don't go so fast! Those cubs aren't going anywhere!"

"Come on! I can see the den now!" Doug yelled back, waving for the others to follow him. "Hey, there's someone outside the den, let's get him! He must be stealing our cubs!"

As soon as he was spotted by the poachers, Knocker took off running into the woods, banging into branches, making a lot of noise, trying to get the men to follow him. Two of the three men followed, but the third stopped by the den.

"Let me just make sure he didn't leave anything behind!" Doug yelled to the others.

Suddenly, a loud roar filled the forest, echoing through the trees. The two men stopped running and turned back to Doug for further directions.

"Doug," one yelled, "there must be another tiger here. Do you want to get it first?"

"Yes, I heard it!" Doug shouted back as he ran towards the other men. "It must be a big one, I've never heard a roar like that before! What a prize! Let's get it!"

Sara scooted back further in the den, as far as she could go, holding the bag with the cubs close. "It's okay," she whispered softly, "I'm still here, I won't leave you alone!"

Soft whimpers from inside the bag revealed the cubs were doing their best to be quiet, but they were very scared.

"Listen, as soon as we can, I'm going to take us out of this den and into the forest, so the poachers won't find us when they come back, you are safe with me!" she called to them softly.

Sara heard the roaring continue for several more minutes, it was running away from the den. The men's shouting got further away as they chased whatever was making the noise.

"Okay, little ones, my name is Sara and I'm here to help," she said softly, opening the bag to peek in. There was very little light reflecting from the den opening; she could only make out a little movement in the bottom of the bag. "Stay still while I get out of the den, and then we can get away, okay?"

"Yes, Sara," said one cub very faintly, his voice shaking with fear. "My name is Nikolas, and my sister Stella and brother Thomas are here. Thank you for helping us. We were so scared when our mom had to leave us, I am so glad you and Knocker came to help!"

"I'll keep you all safe, Nikolas, I promise," Sara said, hoping to reassure him.

Crawling slowly on her hands and knees as she kept the bag over one shoulder, Sara was able to get to the den opening. She stopped to listen carefully, the shouting was far in the distance; however, she couldn't hear the roaring anymore. She hoped whatever they were chasing got away!

Taking hold of her necklace, she hoped that its magic would last through the night, and it would help guide her and these little tiger cubs to safety. It was not safe in the den!

After a few moments, the voice came to her. "It is safe to leave now, go quickly and quietly to the west, there should be enough moonlight to see the ground, and I will guide you to a safe place."

That is all that Sara needed to hear. Quickly standing up and getting a firm hold on the bag, she turned to the west.

"Hold on, little buddies!" she whispered as she started her way through the trees. She could see enough to move forward through the small trees and rocks, and the area to the west was hilly. They could hide behind one of the hills until it was safe for Knocker to return and find them.

"Keep heading in this direction, towards the large trees," Sara heard the voice call to her. She looked forward but wasn't sure if she was heading in the right direction, she looked around in the darkness, trying to find a point to head towards. "Follow the moon, it is heading west!"

Sara thought for a moment, what is it trying to tell me? Then it made perfect sense, the moon rises in the east and sets in the west. The moon would tell her what direction to go! She headed towards the moon—that would keep her on track and away from the road. She didn't want to get lost and accidently circle back to the road where the poachers had parked their truck!

The landscape was changing, there were now hilly slopes and larger trees. She looked around, trying to find somewhere that might be a good place to hide. She could hear the shouting of the men again; they were heading back to the den. She must go faster! She started to run but stopped suddenly when the voice called out to her. "Sounds may reveal you and your friends!"

Crouching quickly close to the ground, Sara looked behind her. Had the poachers heard her? She was afraid to move now, afraid that they would see her. Clasping her necklace in her hand, she waited for some further instruction, for the calm she needed to feel inside. She would not move until the voice told her it was safe!

"Slow and quiet, keep yourself low, like a tiger!" Sara got quietly off the ground, but stayed bent over, holding the duffle bag with its precious cargo close to her chest. "Hang in there, little buddies, we'll get through this together!" she whispered quietly, hoping her voice sounded calm and didn't reveal the nervousness she felt inside.

"Behind the next hill, there is a small cave, go inside!" Sara moved as quickly as she dared, going behind the hill, and once hidden from sight of anyone to the east, she stood and ran into the cave. Now all she could do was wait, and hope Knocker could find them!

LOST IN THE WOODS

Sara went as far back into the cave as she dared, but she needed to see the entrance, the small opening of light from the moon. There she sat in the darkness, just outside of the moonbeams shining into the cave, able to see but not be seen! Holding the duffle bag close, she whispered to the cubs, "We are safe now, we just need to wait for our friend Knocker to come back!"

Sara did not share with them the slow panic that was rising in her; her fear that Knocker would not be able to find them in the dark, or worse, that he had been caught by the poachers. She reached for her necklace, hoping it would once again give her calm, letting her know things would be okay. Focusing on the necklace, she did feel its calmness spreading through her. It was like this tiger's claw had a spirit, and it could connect with her, if only she would let it in.

Since her mom died several years ago, it was hard for Sara to let anyone in, trust anyone enough to even talk about more than just cooking or the weather. The illness that took her mom away wasn't visible on the outside, her mom just got weaker and weaker, until she was unable to move out of bed anymore.

Hiding her illness from her dad because they didn't have money for medicine, her mom kept saying she would be fine soon, but she only got worse. When her dad and brother finally realized she was not getting any better, it was too late. She passed away several days later in her sleep. Her last words to Sara were, "I love you, little one, take care of yourself!"

Those words came back to Sara now as she sat in the dark shadows of the cave, hoping that Knocker would find her. The words had been her only strength, knowing that she had her mom's love. Over the past two years, she grew determined to take care of herself and not let anything keep her from doing what was right, even rescuing tiger cubs from poachers! Holding the bag with the little cubs tight, she whispered, "Don't worry, little ones, I will keep you safe!"

After a few minutes in the darkness, the voice in the necklace spoke to her again, giving her encouragement. "Knocker is on his way back; he will be here soon!" One hand holding the necklace, and the other hand hugging the bag with the cubs, she waited for Knocker's return.

Footsteps outside of the cave caused Sara to catch her breath—who was it? Was it Knocker, or was it the poachers? She slipped quietly further back into the cave's darkness, and waited, listening to the footsteps as they got closer. The person outside stopped and stood still for a few moments, then looked in the cave.

"Sara, are you here?" Knocker whispered softly, "I'm back now."

"Yes, Knocker, I'm here." Sara whispered back, still fearful of any loud noises giving their location away.

Kneeling and entering the cave, Knocker made his way over to Sara and the cubs and sat down beside her. "Are you and the cubs okay?"

"Yes, I'm fine, thanks for coming back!" Sara replied. Then she opened the top of the bag and said to them, "Hey, little ones, are you okay?"

Nikolas popped his head out, saying in a brave voice, "I'm good. Stella and Thomas are scared, but I am protecting them!"

"Knocker, this probably isn't the time, but can you please explain why you and I can talk to these cubs?" Sara asked, still trying to figure this out in her head.

Knocker nodded and replied, "Well, Sara, where I live, things are a bit different than here. We have what humans consider magic." Reaching into a pocket in the large bag, he pulled out a small flat stone. "This is what we call a translation stone. It allows humans to speak with non-humans. It has a range of about ten feet from the stone. Since it was in the bag, you were able to talk to the cubs while you were holding the bag."

"That's amazing!" Sara whispered. "Where do you live?"

"I live far away from here." Knocker said, then his voice got serious as he continued. "I was sent here on a mission, to save some cubs that had been caught and caged; the poachers are going to take them over the border tonight, to sell to the highest bidder. I want to stop them and rescue the cubs. When I saw you out earlier, I knew it was too dangerous for you to be in the forest tonight, as the poachers are in this area getting their cargo ready."

"Once I heard of your mission, I knew we had to rescue these cubs also." Knocker continued. "However, I will get you home before I complete my mission, and I will take these three little cubs with me so they will be safe."

"Thank you for rescuing the cubs," Sara replied. "I hope one day to be brave enough to help the animals in the area. Now I can only watch as poachers kill and capture our native wildlife, stealing whatever they can and paying off the border guards to sell far away. Between the poachers and the logging destroying the animals' homes, there aren't many animals left."

"Thank you, Sara," Knocker said. "Know that it is courage and spirit that can save these animals, and you have both. You came out tonight, knowing you could get caught, to help a mother save her babies. You are already brave enough!"

"But now we need to get you back to your house before you are missed, and I need to rescue these cubs and get on with my mission," Knocker said as he stood and started towards the cave entrance. "It's important that the poachers don't associate you with the cubs, your role in this rescue must remain a secret, okay?"

"Of course, anything to keep them safe!" Sara replied.

The sound of a gunshot and human voices shouting echoed through the area, causing them both to freeze at the entrance to the cave. These voices sounded different though, there must be another group of poachers!

"I think we got it!" the man yelled as he started running in the direction of the cave.

Chapter Six

A SECOND ATTACK

"**S**ara," Knocker whispered urgently, "You must take the cubs and go back into the cave. Let me find out what has happened!"

Nodding quickly and holding the bag with the cubs tight, she went back into the darkness, hiding away from the poachers. She heard Knocker running into the forest, then heard roaring and growling in the distance. She also heard shouting and people running in the underbrush, but she didn't budge from the back wall of cave, she had to keep the cubs safe.

A few minutes later Knocker appeared at the entrance to the cave, she could see him in the moon light, and he was holding something. "Sara, come out quickly with the cubs!" he whispered softly but urgently into the cave.

As Sara exited from the cave, she saw Knocker in the moonlight; he was holding a young tiger in his arms. The tiger's leg was bleeding, he had been shot!

"There is a second group of poachers in the area, Sara, and they are also hunting tigers tonight!"

Knocker said quickly. "This is Manuel, he has been shot in the leg. He will not be able to get away from the poachers and needs a healer's attention. I cannot leave him to the poachers—I need to get him away from here now!"

"I understand and agree, Knocker, you must save him." Sara replied nodding her head in agreement, still holding the cubs. "What should we do while you are gone?"

"Sara, I need your courage and spirit now," said Knocker seriously as he looked into her eyes. "I need to take Manuel and the cubs, get them to safety away from the poachers in the forest tonight. It will not take long, and then I will be back for you to make sure you get home safely."

"Can you stay hidden in the cave while I'm gone?" Knocker said as he looked at her, hoping she would understand he needed to leave her once again. "You will be safer there, as I must travel quickly!"

Looking at the tiger in his arms, Sara knew it needed help now, she could stay in the cave for a bit longer while Knocker took it to safety. She had her necklace to keep her calm. "Yes, Knocker, you must rescue these tigers. As you told me before, I am brave enough! I will wait for you in the cave!" She hoped she sounded braver than she was feeling right now.

She handed the bag with the cubs to him, helping him get the bag's strap onto his shoulder as he gently held the other tiger. Then she turned and went quickly to the entrance of the cave, calling to him, "Hurry, Knocker, before you are caught!"

"Thank you!" Knocker said, "Don't come out for any reason. I will be back very soon!"

Sara watched from the front of the cave as she saw Knocker running away carrying the wounded tiger and the bag with the cubs. As soon as he was out of sight, she heard a loud roar, and she feared they had been caught by the poachers. However, the roar was followed quickly by a flash of blue light. She wasn't sure what was going on out there, possibly the light was from the poachers using searchlights to find the tiger.

That was her signal to go back into the cave and hide. She found some large rocks to block her from view if someone looked in the cave. Holding tight to her necklace, she hoped that it would keep her calm as she waited for Knocker to return.

Voices were getting closer to the cave, and Sara crouched close to the ground behind the rocks.

"Did you see that light? It must be someone who found our tiger, let's get him!" one shouted.

"Wayne," shouted another, "I see some tiger paw prints, and some human footprints here; I think you're right. You must have shot the tiger, and someone has taken him!"

"Follow the footprints!" Wayne shouted. "Don't let him get away!"

The sound of running footsteps, along with the crackling of leaves and branches on the forest floor, echoed through the trees, getting louder as the men approached the cave. They were heading this way!

"Hey, Wayne," called the closest man. "Come look over here!"

"Yeah, Rory," Wayne replied as he got closer to the cave, "What did you find?"

"It looks like footprints; the guy must have been here. I don't see any tiger prints though," Rory said as he shined his flashlight on the ground in front of the cave. "Let me check in here."

Rory walked over to the entrance and shined his flashlight into the cave. Sara stayed motionless, holding her breath, and clutching her necklace in her hand, hoping they would go away. She didn't dare move—they might see or hear her!

"I don't see anything in there, Wayne," Rory said. "I wonder where they could have gone!"

Suddenly, a loud roaring sound could be heard in the distance.

"There's the tiger!" Wayne shouted. "He's still alive, he must have gotten away! Let's go!" Wayne and Rory raced towards the roar and away from the cave.

Sara stayed motionless; nothing was going to get her to move until she heard Knocker's voice again. She could not trust that all the poachers had left, what if it was a trap to get her to come out of the cave?

"Be calm!" The voice from the necklace was calling to her. "Knocker has returned and will be here soon!"

Chapter Seven

AN
UNEXPECTED JOURNEY

S ara heard footsteps outside of the cave again, heading her way. Stopping outside, the footsteps paused for a few seconds, then someone leaned over and called into the cave.

"Sara," Knocker called quietly. "I'm back! Are you okay?"

"Is it safe to come out now?" she whispered back.

"Yes, Sara, come on out, it is safe—for now. However, we will have to figure out how to get you home," Knocker said.

As Sara crawled out of the cave, she stood and looked at Knocker and asked, "Did you get the cubs and Manuel to safety?" She hoped he had been successful in escaping the poachers.

"Yes, all have been transported to an island where Manuel will receive care for his injuries. We are also arranging for another tiger to adopt the three little cubs." Knocker replied. "Thank you for your help in the rescue, we are very grateful!"

"That is great to hear! How can I get back home?" Sara asked. "What way is clear?"

"There are now two bands of poachers out there. They are working against each other; one is trying to steal the cubs I'm trying to rescue from the other." Knocker replied. "Both groups are shooting at anything that moves in the forest tonight!"

"So, what are we going to do?" Sara wondered. "Which way can we go?"

"If I remember correctly, Wayne's group is to the north, and Doug's group is south, so if we go east and past the den again, we may be able to sneak between the two of them." Knocker said as he was trying to think things out. "However, if they head towards each other, we could get caught in the middle. Another option would be to head west until we are away from Doug's group and then head south in the woods until we get even with your house, then turn east."

"Where is the cage with the little cubs you need to rescue? Who has them?" Sara asked, remembering Knocker's original mission in the area before he came to rescue her.

"From what I saw earlier, the cage is even with the stopped vehicle in the road on the west side. The poachers who are taking the cubs over the border tonight is Doug's group, that's why they parked there. That would put it to the northwest of your house," Knocker responded.

"So, we need to get me home as quickly as possible, and you can complete your mission to rescue the caged cubs and get away too, right?" Sara said. "What if we try going east now, if the two bands of poachers are separated?"

"Let's go then!" Knocker agreed, heading east. "We can go east until we get to the den and then cross the road and return to your house the way we got here."

Moving quickly through the underbrush and trees, Knocker and Sara arrived back at the den. They passed by quietly on the way to the road; pausing at the road to look for signs of either group of poachers before trying to cross.

Sara put her hand on her necklace, seeking help from the voice that had guided her before. She asked it softly, "Are we safe to cross the road now?" Then she waited for a response. After a few moments, she heard it reply. "They are coming your way from both sides!"

"Knocker, the voice says that the poachers are approaching from both sides, we must be caught in the middle!" Sara whispered urgently. "What can we do?"

"Let's head back the way we came; they must be trying to get to the den!" Knocker said as he turned back towards the hilly forest. "Let's go to the cave and head north, maybe we can circle back around and get to the road that way!"

Knocker took Sara's hand and ran swiftly through the forest. Sara was having trouble seeing because of the darkness, but it didn't appear to bother Knocker.

He was able to lead them back to the cave in just a few minutes.

"Okay, let's go north here, Wayne's group should be trying to find Doug's group to the south. If we stay north of Wayne's group, we should be okay," Knocker said, heading north through a hilly section of the forest.

Knocker stopped for a moment and took a deep breath, then looked to the south. "We aren't far enough north. We may not be able to get past the second group!"

"Sara, again I must ask you to be brave. Do you trust me?" Knocker said quietly.

"Yes, I do, Knocker. I know you are doing your best to protect me and the animals. I trust you," Sara replied. "What do you need from me?"

"We are trapped in this area. I cannot let you be seen by the poachers; it will be dangerous for you and your entire family!" Knocker said. "I will need to ask for help transporting us out of this situation. But if we are transported out, you may see some things that you can't share with anyone else, even your own family. Will you agree to keep my secrets?"

Sara was not sure what secrets Knocker might have, but he was courageously rescuing the animals in the area and trying to get her home safely. She would do whatever she could to help him. "Yes," Sara replied. "I will keep whatever secrets you might reveal, I promise!"

"Thank you, Sara," Knocker said. "Please stay close to me!"

Knocker turned to look at the sky, in the direction of the moon, and called out loudly, "Guardian, we need your help now!"

Sara looked around to see who he might be calling to, but she could see no one. A few seconds later, a large column of blue light flashed, surrounding her and Knocker, and she felt herself being lifted in the air, speeding towards the sky. As she looked around, she felt lightheaded and dizzy, and could not focus on what was happening. Within a few seconds, she was unconscious.

Chapter Eight

MEETING ITURIA

Sara was slowly regaining consciousness; she could hear voices around her, but she was still too sleepy to open her eyes.

"… doesn't know about you, correct, Knocker?" a voice asked.

"That is correct, Ituria. She knows about the translation stone, and we used it to speak to the tiger cubs." Knocker said, then added, "There are two groups of poachers at odds with each other. I highly suspect the second group may be planning to steal the cubs I'm rescuing from the first group."

"You will need to wake her so you can get back," Ituria said. "Guardian will have another generate the vortex, so you can get the girl home."

"I agree, Ituria. She does have a necklace that speaks to her, though, and it was very helpful in rescuing the tiger cubs earlier," Knocker replied. "I would like you to view it, as possibly you can determine what is happening when she talks to it. I have not seen this phenomenon before."

"Do you have time now, or should we wait for another opportunity?" Ituria asked.

"I would like to investigate further; however, we only have a few minutes now. Will that be enough time if she will share it with you for a moment or two?" Knocker replied quietly. "I need to get her home so I can complete my mission, as the caged cubs I need to rescue will be transported some-time tonight."

"I agree, Knocker, you need to get her home safely." Ituria looked over to where Sara was laying, and added, "She seems to be awake now, though. Perhaps we will have a few minutes to talk." Ituria said as he moved closer, and Sara heard pebbles scattering as he walked across the room.

"Sara, are you awake now?" Knocker said as he touched her gently on the shoulder. "We have to get you back to your home soon!"

Sara opened her eyes and looked around her, trying to figure out exactly where they were. "Where are we? Who are you talking to?" she asked sleepily as she looked around the room.

"Greetings, Sara, I am pleased to meet you," Ituria said. "Welcome to my island home!"

Sara had been laying on the ground, but she sat up quickly when she saw Ituria. A tall white horse with flowing white mane and a golden horn on his forehead was talking to her! *Am I dreaming?* "Are you speaking to me?" she asked in amaze-ment, "Are you real?"

"Yes, Sara, I am real. Knocker brought you to my island to keep you safe. I'm afraid you will have to return soon, though, before you are missed," Ituria replied in a friendly voice.

"Are you … a unicorn?" Sara asked, still stunned by what she was seeing in front of her.

"Yes, I am, and you are on my island, we call it Ituria's Island," Ituria said. "Our mission is to rescue animals who are being treated cruelly by humans. I want to thank you for aiding Knocker tonight, helping him rescue the three cubs and the young tiger, Manuel."

"How did we get here? I remember a blue light flash, and then I must have passed out," Sara said, still trying to get a grasp of what had happened.

"We have a way to transport animals and humans to our island that is controlled by Guardian. He will need to return you soon. However, Knocker mentioned that you have a necklace that speaks to you. Is that true?" Ituria asked.

Sara looked quickly at Knocker, her eyes wide and frightened. Even in these most extraordinary of circumstances, she still was scared to let anyone see it. "Well, it was something my father gave to me," Sara said softly, covering the necklace with her hand.

"Do you know why or how it talks to you?" Ituria asked. "You don't have to share if you don't want, as it is your necklace, and we would not do anything that would make you uncomfortable."

"Well, I don't know how it works," Sara replied. "It just talks to me when I hold it in my hand. Like it knows what I am asking in my mind, and it gives me an answer. I know it sounds crazy, but it has been a crazy night tonight, so it fits right in, right?"

"Can you show it to us?" Ituria asked. "I am curious as to how it works."

"Well, I think I can share it with you, just for a moment," Sara responded slowly. "But then we need to get home, my father may be looking for me."

"Agreed, Sara," Knocker responded. "We will need to get you home soon. It was just that your relationship with your necklace is something I have never seen before. I thought Ituria might have heard of it before."

"So, when I am worried, I hold it in my hand, like this." Sara said, wrapping her fingers around the claw on the necklace. "And it gives me calmness to think, it calms my panic. Knocker said it was the source of the other voice, that the necklace was channeling another being, but I don't understand what happened tonight. And I think the eye thing was just the moon."

"But there is no moon light shining here, Sara, and I can see your eyes have changed. Do you feel it?" Knocker asked. "Ituria, do you see it also?"

"Yes, Knocker," Ituria replied with a little surprise. "If you are referring to the change in Sara's eyes, I can see it too. It is indeed unusual."

"What are you talking about, what do you see?" Sara asked, worried about what they were seeing, what was happening to her eyes that caused them to notice?

"Your eyes change to the eyes of a tiger, Sara," Ituria responded. "Do you know why?"

Chapter Nine

ANGELA INTRODUCES HERSELF

Sara closed her eyes and clutched the necklace tight, holding it to her chest. She was getting scared now; she needed the calmness now that her necklace has provided over the past few weeks. What were Knocker and Ituria seeing?

"Sara," Ituria said as he noticed she was getting upset. "Why don't we leave this conversation for another time? It has been a long night, and we still must get you home and let Knocker complete his mission. We can talk again once all of this is behind us."

"Thank you, Ituria," Sara said, breathing a sigh of relief. "I am still not sure what is going on with this necklace; my father gave it to me a few weeks ago and told me not to let anyone know about it."

"I understand, and I would not want you to feel nervous or threatened," Ituria replied. "Your father was right, it is a valuable gift for you, it belongs to you, and you should only talk about it when you are ready."

"It may make a lot more sense in the morning. Thank you again," Sara said, then turned to Knocker. "When will we be able to return home?"

"We can go now, Sara, and I will get you back to your house safely. I've talked with Guardian so he can drop us close to the back of your house," Knocker replied.

Sara reached up and held her necklace again, ready for the calmness that followed. But instead, she heard a message that required immediate attention instead. "The poachers are approaching your house; you must return before they get there!"

"Knocker!" Sara exclaimed. "The voice says the poachers are on their way to my house, we must hurry!"

"Sara, ask the voice who she is," Ituria asked quickly. "Tell it that we want to help it in any way we can but need to know who it is first."

Sara closed her eyes and held the necklace tight. Would it understand what Ituria was asking? Did it want to reveal itself? What if it left and never returned because she had revealed it to others? Fear crept into Sara's mind, maybe she should not disturb the spirit that spoke through the necklace! Then the calmness returned. "Do not fear, Sara, these beings can be trusted. I will answer their questions. But we must be quick to get you home!"

Sara slowly released the necklace and a whisp of smoke floated up from the tiger claw. It grew larger and larger until it was a small vaporous cloud, encircling Sara's shoulders—the spirit needed to stay connected to the necklace!

"I am Angela," said a soft voice slowly—sounding like an echo. "I was killed by humans. I remained behind as my body was taken away, staying with this small part of me that was left behind. I hope to save other animals from suffering the same fate, and my spirit watches over the forest and its creatures. Tonight, I saw a mother tiger being shot by the poachers and focused her calls for help through the necklace so that Sara could hear them, so that her cubs could be rescued!"

"Thank you, Angela." Knocker said softly with respect. "With your help and Sara's help, we were able to save the three cubs that had been orphaned. They are now here and will be taken care of by another tiger mother. They will never have to worry about being hunted by humans again."

"Angela," Ituria began, "I can feel that your courage and spirit are great, and we sincerely appreciate your actions to protect other animals. Please know that you are always welcome to stay on my island should you desire to do so."

"I am glad that you were able to make a connection with young Sara," Ituria continued. "Sara also has courage and spirit, as she has shown tonight! Can you please accompany her home, so she is safe?"

"Sara has a good spirit in her. She is a caring human, and I will be glad to help her get home," Angela said softly, but urgency crept into her echoing voice as she continued. "We need to go soon, please.

The poachers are looking for someone, and she needs to be home when they get to her house!"

"Then we will return immediately!" Knocker replied as he stood and walked over to Sara. "Sara, please accompany me to the opening there, and we will have Guardian send us back now. I have already arranged the location with him."

The small billowy cloud surrounding Sara that was Angela's spirit thinned and faded into a thread of smoke as it returned to the tiger claw. Angela was ready to return! Holding the necklace tight, Sara said, "Okay, Knocker, I'm ready; let's go!"

As Knocker and Sara moved to a clear area, Ituria said, "Best of luck on your mission, Knocker. We will await your return. And thank you Angela and young Sara, for all your help!"

Once Knocker and Sara were in position, Knocker called out loudly, "Guardian, we are ready!"

A blue beam of light focused on them, and suddenly they were on their way back to Sara's home. Sara tried to stay awake during the journey to figure out how the blue beam of light was involved; however, she was soon fast asleep.

She awoke to the sound of Knocker calling to her softly, "Sara, we are back now, let's get you home!"

Chapter Ten

RETURNING HOME

K nocker helped Sara to her feet, and then looked around, trying to get an idea of who might still be the forest around them. He had his duffle bag with him, ready for the second set of cubs to be rescued.

"I can hear something, but it sounds far away," Knocker whispered. "Let's see if we can get you home. It should only be a short distance west of here. I had Guardian transport us away from where the poachers were roaming around."

"Thanks, Knocker," Sara replied. "It is dark and hard to see, so we'll need to stick close together."

With Knocker leading the way, they walked quickly through the forest towards her home. Knocker paused as they were close to the house and pulled Sara behind a tree.

Pointing to the road in front of her house, he whispered, "Sara, it looks like there is a group of poachers standing outside your house."

As they stood hiding behind the tree, the voices of the poachers carried through the night air as they shouted to each other. Two of them were about twenty feet apart and facing different directions, one north and one south, watching the road. The third was standing in between and looking at Sara's house.

"You keep looking to the north, okay Rory?" said a voice.

"Yep, and you watch the south, Blane," said Rory. "We need to make sure that guy doesn't get away! We also need to find Doug's group—remember they have a cage full of cubs that Wayne wants us to acquire! Right, Wayne?" Rory chuckled and added. "I hope the *acquiring* goes smoothly!"

The third poacher turned and started walking towards Sara's house, looking around as he approached the door. "I'll only be a few minutes, just making sure the local residents are safe!"

"Wayne, what do you need from this house, anyway?" Blane asked.

"I just want to make sure the residents weren't helping that guy that left footprints near the cave earlier, and that everyone from this house is inside tonight!" Wayne said as he stopped and called over to Blane in a menacing voice. "It wouldn't be good for any of the logger families to be out tonight—it's too dangerous. We might have to report them to the authorities for breaking curfew!"

Rory laughed at Wayne's comment and added, "My brother would make sure something was done if they didn't stay inside at night like they were told. It would be bad luck for them!"

Wayne turned and started heading for the house again, still glancing around as he went up the walkway, to make sure there was no one in the forest around the home.

"Knocker," Sara whispered urgently, "did you hear that? The leader of the first group is heading to my house, I need to get home now!"

"You won't be able to get in the front, is there a way in the back you can sneak in before he reaches the house?" Knocker asked.

"Yes, I'm on my way!" Sara whispered, as she started running through the forest to the back door, the moon giving just enough light here to maneuver through the trees.

"I will wait out back until the poachers are gone and will come to help if you call for me!" Knocker said, following her so he could position himself in the back yard once she got into the house. "I won't leave you in danger!"

Sara slipped in the back door and listened to find out if Wayne was inside the house yet. She heard a loud knock on the front door, and her father called out, "Who's out there at this time of night?"

"I need to make sure everyone is okay inside!" Wayne called loudly. "Let me in!"

"We are fine, everyone is sleeping, please go away!" Sara's father replied, his voice fearful of this man banging on the door.

"No, you must let me in, the authorities have asked me to check all homes to make sure all residents are inside. Don't make me break the door down!" Wayne's voice was very loud and demanding;

he was coming into the house whether he was allowed or not!

Sara slipped off her shoes and walked into the main room of the house. Her bed was in a small room near the kitchen, close to the back door, so her father would think she was coming from her room.

"Father, what's going on?" she called out, letting him know she was awake and in the front room. "Who is banging on the door?"

"Sara, go back to your room now and stay there!" her father ordered. "Don't come out when these men are here, okay?"

"Yes, Father!" she said anxiously, then she turned and ran to her room, climbing into bed and pulling the bed covers over her.

After her father opened the front door, Wayne walked in the main living area and looked around. "Is everyone home tonight?" he asked brashly. "I'm to check to make sure."

"Yes, my son and daughter are sleeping. We are all here in the house, no one has gone out!" he replied.

"Well, I heard the little girl a minute ago, but I didn't hear the boy. Wake him up so I can make sure he isn't outside somewhere. We have seen a dangerous criminal prowling the forest tonight, so we need to confirm everyone is safe!"

"Samuel!" her father called out. "Get up and come out here now!"

As Samuel came slowly out of one of the rooms, he looked around frantically, scared by this intrusion. "What's wrong, Father? What's happening?" he said in a frightened voice.

"Okay, boy, we just needed to make sure you were home, now go back to bed!" Wayne shouted at him rudely. "Everyone needs to stay inside tonight, understand?" Wayne ordered in a nasty voice as he turned and walked out, slamming the door behind him.

Chapter Eleven

LATE NIGHT DISCUSSION

After Wayne left, Sara's father called from the front room, "Sara and Samuel, you are safe now—they have gone away!" His voice was filled with relief that they were safe, at least for now.

He walked into Sara's small room and gave her a hug. "No need to worry anymore tonight, they are gone." Looking at her quizzically, he asked, "You still have your day clothes on, Sara. Why is that?"

"Yes, Father, I was cold, so just stayed in my day clothes when I went to sleep tonight. They are warmer," Sara replied, hoping her father wouldn't question her further.

"Okay, little one," her father responded with deep affection. "Here's another hug to keep you warm!" He gave her a big hug and then tucked her into bed. "Your brother and I will be leaving early in the morning again, so please stay safe in the house, okay? There's a lot of people roaming the forest now."

"I'll be safe, Father," Sara replied. "Remember, I have the necklace you gave me to keep me safe!"

"You must keep that hidden, remember?" her father said, panic creeping into his voice. "If those poachers saw you with that necklace, there is no telling what they would do!"

"Yes, Father. I will make sure to always keep it hidden, I promise!" Sara replied. "It means so much to me, I am glad that you found it for me! Thank you!" Sara jumped up and gave her father another hug and then lay back down in her bed, pulling a blanket over her.

Sara listened as her father went to talk to Samuel, calming him down and getting him back to sleep. Although Samuel was only fourteen, he worked just as hard as her father did for the logging company, so they could earn enough money to keep their house.

As soon as the house was quiet and Sara was sure her father had gone back to bed, she slipped her shoes back on and went quietly out the back door.

"Knocker," she whispered, "are you still here?"

"Yes, Sara, I am here," Knocker said softly as he appeared close enough for Sara to see him in the moonlight. "I needed to make sure you are safe before I can continue on my mission."

"Did you hear what the poachers said earlier?" Sara asked. "They are looking for the boy who left the footprints by the cave."

"No, I didn't hear; what else did they say—anything about the cubs?" Knocker asked.

"Yes, this was Wayne's group," Sara answered. "And they are planning on stealing the cubs from the other group tonight. You will be facing both this group and the original group." Sara looked at Knocker and continued anxiously. "That may be too much for one person, Knocker, even you! Is there any way Angela and I can help? If you get caught between these two groups, there may be no way out for you—or the cubs!"

"Let's think this through, Sara. As you noted, it is going to be a perilous mission tonight. I will have to rescue four cubs from a locked cage with two separate bands of poachers trying to stop me," Knocker explained seriously. "I'm not sure if there is a solution at this point."

"What if you let Angela and I talk to the cubs? It would keep them calm," Sara suggested. "If you can break the lock on the cage, I can climb in and grab them and put them into your bag."

"Sara, there is something I do need to tell you," Knocker said with slight hesitation. "You know how Angela talks to you through the claw necklace?"

"Yes, she told us that while we were with Ituria," Sara replied, wondering why Knocker would bring that up now. "Why?"

"Well, I can talk to the cubs, and they will understand me." Knocker said. "Did you know non-humans can understand each other's languages? Different species can talk to each other, and it is only humans who can't understand non-humans."

"You have the translation stone, right? You said that allowed you to talk to the cubs earlier," Sara said, still trying to figure out where Knocker was going with this conversation.

"Well, yes," Knocker agreed, "I do have a translation stone." Knocker paused for a moment, then continued quietly as he looked into Sara's eyes. "I use the translation stone to allow me to talk to you."

Chapter Twelve

MAKING A PLAN

"**W**hy do you need it to talk to me?" Sara asked, confused by what Knocker was trying to tell her.

"I am not what I appear to be, Sara," Knocker explained. "I need to tell you this in case I must change into my natural form tonight. If I do, please do not be frightened. You need to realize that if we figure out a plan that will rescue the cubs, I will protect you from anyone who would try to harm you, no matter what."

"Knocker, you are frightening me now," Sara said anxiously. "What are you talking about?"

"Just remember that I will protect you, okay?" Knocker repeated. "Now let's see what plan we can make. It is almost midnight now, so we only have an hour or two until the cubs are leaving, based on what I overheard Doug's group say. And if Wayne is planning on stealing the cubs, they may already be at or near the cage."

"It might be the best solution for me to open the cage and let you crawl in to get the cubs. You will have the translation stone, so you can tell them to be quiet and that we are rescuing them," Knocker said. "This way, I can stay alert for the poachers and distract them from the cage. You can talk to Angela too, as she will be able to alert us to any danger."

"One more thing, Sara," Knocker said quietly, trying to keep Sara calm. "If you are to help me with my mission to rescue these cubs, I need you to take a magic potion that will make you invisible, will you do that?"

"What?" Sara asked incredulously. What else could possibly happen tonight? "Why do I need to be invisible?"

"If you are going to go into the cage and rescue the cubs, the invisibility spell will make them invisible also, if you are holding them. This way the poachers won't have a chance to see you or the cubs, even if they see me," Knocker explained. "It will wear off in a few hours; however, this is important to keep you and the cubs safe."

"If you want to help me and the cubs," Knocker continued, his voice stressed. "This is the only way I can let you go with me. I cannot let you be seen by these poachers for any reason, it is too dangerous for you and your family!" Sara could tell he was still deciding whether he should allow her to join him on his dangerous mission.

"I'll do it!" Sara replied with determination, knowing that Knocker would need help to rescue the caged cubs. "I will take the invisibility potion, there is too much at stake, too many obstacles for you alone!"

Nodding once to acknowledge her decision, Knocker reached into his bag, pulling out a small glass bottle with liquid inside. "Thank you for your help, Sara," he said in a serious tone. "I will need all the help I can get to be successful tonight. You need to drink about half of this bottle, it will start working within a few seconds, so don't move while you are drinking it."

Looking at Knocker, Sara nodded back in agreement and reached out for the small bottle. Half of the contents would only be about an ounce, maybe one mouthful. She put her finger around the bottle to mark where half of it would be, and then took a drink. Quickly looking at the bottle, she saw that she had it just about right, so she didn't need to drink anymore. Then she watched as her hand and the small bottle faded into the darkness of the night. She was invisible!

"Good work, Sara!" Knocker whispered with enthusiasm. "Now put the bottle on the ground so I can pick it up and put it back in my bag, and let's go rescue the cubs!"

"Sara, one more important point," Knocker whispered to where Sara was last visible. "I will be the distraction, if needed, while you rescue the cubs, okay?"

"Okay, Knocker," Sara responded anxiously, concerned for his safety, "I agree—but only if you make sure you are safe too. Remember, I can't get the cubs to Ituria's Island, only you can."

"Sara, listen," Knocker explained in the direction of her voice. "You *can* go to Ituria's Island. If something does happen to me, remember how we got out last time. Shout as loud as you can into the sky at the moon—'Guardian, I need your help!'—okay? If I tell you to do that, you must do so immediately."

"I am to shout at the moon? Why?" Sara asked, this night was getting crazier by the minute.

"Ituria's Island is on the moon. Guardian is watching us now, so if you shout to him, he will hear you and will take you and the cubs to safety." Knocker's voice was stressed. "It's important that you remember, okay?"

"I will remember, but you said you would be safe, so I will trust that you will keep me and the cubs safe!" Sara said, this was just one more incredible issue that didn't make any sense. Ituria—a unicorn—lives on the moon? I'm invisible! Tomorrow this may all make sense, but tonight, she just wanted to get to the cubs and get away from the poachers as soon as possible.

"Can Guardian see me if I am invisible? And can he rescue us both if you are in trouble and I call to him?" Sara asked quickly as many questions started popping into her head.

"Guardian will hear you and direct the beam in your direction, transporting you and the cubs if you are holding them. However, Guardian will not transport me until I am ready and call to him myself," Knocker replied quickly, anxious to get the mission started. "We must get the cubs to the moon and you back home before the invisibility potion wears off. Are you ready?"

"Yes, I'm ready!" Sara answered.

"Okay, let's be on our way, I'm hoping to beat the poachers back to their camp!" Knocker whispered and he headed to the west. "Stay close to me, as I can't see you!"

"Will do!" Sara replied as she followed close behind.

Chapter Thirteen

Rescuing the Cubs

Knocker stopped and looked before crossing the road, making sure he would not be seen, then quickly crossed and went to the woods on the other side. "Are you still with me?" he whispered.

"Yes, I'm next to you on your left!" Sara whispered back.

The forest was thicker in this area; it had not been logged yet, and there were many old-growth trees and thick underbrush. Knowing Knocker could not see her, Sara followed him closely as he made a path through the underbrush, so they wouldn't get separated.

"It looks like an opening up ahead," Knocker whispered as he turned his head towards Sara's voice. "This is where the cubs should be! We must be careful and silent!" Knocker paused and took a deep breath. Then he continued, quietly but urgently, "The poachers are just ahead of us!"

Circling around the opening while keeping out of the sight of the poachers, Knocker pointed to the cage on one side of the clearing, barely visible in the lights from the flashlights of the two poachers in front of them. They stopped just outside the clearing next to the cage and listened closely to the discussion.

"Doug, we got the mom tiger, but her cubs weren't in the den. They must have been taken away by that other group we heard earlier!" a voice called out near the camp. "Good thing we have these cubs, it will make a good sale!"

"Well, Tony," Doug responded with an agitated voice. "Let's start packing up, we need to get out of here. If I know Wayne's group, they heard we were moving some of our goods tonight and they are after them! I'd bet it was Wayne's group that stole the cubs from the den! Remember we saw some guy standing outside the den?"

"Okay, Doug, you may be right," Tony replied. "I'll start getting the truck ready to load the cage over there. I'll need to move things around a bit. We'll be out of here soon, no worries!"

"I always worry until I get my money, Tony!" Doug called back in an agitated voice as Tony turned to leave. "Nothing's guaranteed! Randy should still be at the truck to help get it ready. He was to make sure Wayne's group didn't steal anything from it while we were chasing that tiger!"

As Tony headed east towards the road, Doug sat near a tree about twenty feet away from the cage, using his flashlight to read some papers.

"Hey, Tony," Doug called out as he put the papers back into the backpack. "Wait up and I'll help get the truck ready; we need to get out of here soon!"

Then Doug took off jogging towards the road following Tony.

Once Doug was out of sight, Knocker and Sara got closer to the back of the cage. The clearing allowed for some of the moonlight to show the contents of the large metal cage before them. Sara counted four cubs inside, and they appeared to be sleeping.

Reaching towards the cage, Knocker grabbed two of the metal bars, slowly and quietly bending them apart far enough for Sara to crawl in and reach the cubs. While Knocker's strength surprised Sara, she figured that anything was possible tonight, and she would worry about it all in the morning!

"Sara, take this bag," Knocker said quietly into the night. "If you get them into the bag, then hold the bag next to you, your invisibility spell will work on them too!" Knocker held out the duffle bag, and once Sara took it from his hand and wrapped her arm around it, the bag vanished.

"Wake up little ones, we are here to help you," she whispered to the cubs. But, while she could see the cubs, they could not see her. When they heard the voice without a body, one of the cubs looked up and started whimpering and backing away, scared of what might be in the cage with them.

"It is okay, she is a friend," Knocker whispered to the cub. The cub looked at Knocker, and then to the open space where the bars had been bent and Sara had entered the cage.

"Okay, Knocker," it said with a little more confidence. "If this voice is with you, we will trust her. Please help us get out!"

"Hi, I'm Sara," Sara whispered. "Let me put all of you into this bag so we can get away before the poachers get back, okay?"

"Hi Sara, I am Derek," Derek whispered back to the voice, walking towards it. "Some of the other cubs are weak, so you will need to help them get into the bag, okay?"

Crawling over to the other cubs, Sara could see they were not moving much, but they did turn their heads when they heard her voice, trying to locate the source. "I'm going to help you get out of here, okay?" she said as she picked up each of the other three individually and put them gently into the bag. "Then we can get you some help so you will feel better soon."

"Sara!" Knocker whispered urgently. "I hear someone heading this way. Get out as quickly as possible!"

"Derek!" Sara called softly, "Your turn, let's get you into the bag!"

Derek went towards the voice and allowed Sara to pick him up and put him in the big duffle bag with the others. Turning around quickly, Sara crawled back out of the cage and stood, looking into the night and darkness beyond the clearing, trying to see what might be happening around them. She held the duffle bag full of cubs close to her, so they would be invisible too.

"Good, Sara; you and the bag are invisible, keep hugging the bag to keep them hidden. One of the poacher groups is heading this way, I'm not sure if it is Wayne's group coming to steal the cubs, or Doug's group to move them to the truck!" Knocker whispered to Sara. "It may make a difference to our next move, so I want to wait here a moment to confirm."

Sara watched as Knocker stared into the darkness, taking several deep breaths in different directions. Then he whispered to Sara, "It is Doug's group again—the ones who caught the cubs. They are heading back to move the cage onto the truck! Stay still where you are; I'm going to tell them that Wayne's group stole their cubs."

"What?! You're going to talk to them?" Sara whispered, terrified of Knocker confronting the poachers.

"Yes, if we get them to go after Wayne's group, I can get you home and the cubs back to Ituria's Island," Knocker replied calmly, trying to explain the situation. "They are between us and your house."

"Okay, Knocker, we'll be waiting for you here," Sara whispered anxiously as she stood behind the cage with the bag of cubs, hugging them tightly as she murmured to them. "Please don't make any sounds, we can't let them find you again!"

Knocker walked around to the front of the cage as the voices advanced towards him. After a few moments, the flashlight from one of the men caught Knocker in its beam, and he stopped, waiting for them to say something.

"Hey!" shouted Doug. "What are you doing here? Who are you?"

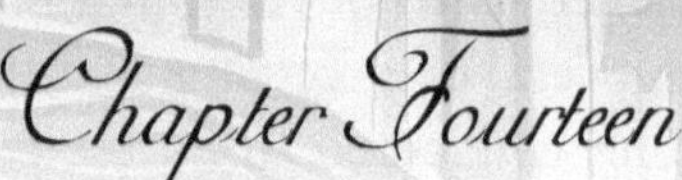

Chapter Fourteen

TRICKING THE POACHERS

"**W**ell, I overheard Wayne say there were some cubs in the woods tonight he wanted to acquire, and I thought I would check it out," Knocker said calmly. "However, the cage is empty."

"What do you mean—the cage is empty!" shouted Doug as he got closer to Knocker, he was only a few feet away now. "And what are you doing here?"

"Tony, go check out the cage—now!" Doug yelled at the man behind him. "And you," Doug shouted as he shined the flashlight in Knocker's face. "You had better explain yourself!"

Tony ran over towards the cage, peeking inside. "He's right, Doug! No cubs left!"

"Look, I overheard Wayne say he was going to acquire your cubs, so I wanted to see what he was talking about. But when I got here, the cage was empty," Knocker replied. "That means Wayne must have taken them before I got here. Nothing here for me now, so I'll be leaving."

Knocker turned to the south, walking next to the now empty cage, and heading out of the clearing. When he was about ten feet away from the men, Knocker turned back and said calmly, "Last time I saw Wayne and his group, they were just a bit to the north of here, around the bend in the road. Maybe you should check it out to see if they are headed back that way. I heard one of them yell they had shot a tiger, so they may have other cubs, too."

"Well, we will just do that!" Doug yelled at him. "And then we'll be back for you! Come on, Tony! Let's get Randy and track them down. We were only gone a few minutes; they can't be too far!"

As Doug and Tony headed off running to the north, Knocker walked slowly around to the back of the cage. He paused for a few seconds to take in several deep breaths of air, and turned towards Sara, finding her location from her scent.

"Sara," Knocker called out softly as he got close to her. "Are you and the cubs okay?"

"Yes, Knocker," she replied, anxious about being out in the woods with two groups of poachers, both wanting the cubs she was holding in the bag. "Let's get these little ones to your island as soon as possible!"

"Agreed, Sara," Knocker replied. "But we need to get you home first, okay? The invisibility spell will last another hour or two, but you should be able to slip in the back door and get to your room and stay there until it wears off. Will that work?"

"Sure," Sara answered. "My father and brother should be sleeping, and I can just hide until I'm visible again. Let's go!"

Heading southeast towards Sara's home, they made it to the road in a few minutes. Before leaving the protection of the trees, Knocker crouched down and peered down the road, looking in both directions. Since Knocker would be visible crossing the road, they wanted to make sure no one else was in the road who might see them. Sara's house was just across the road and a few hundred feet up the drive; they were almost there! Just as Sara started to feel a sense of relief, Angela called to her. "There is someone behind you, be careful!"

Knocker stood up was just about to cross the road when Sara put her hand on his arm to stop him. "No, Knocker," she whispered in a nervous voice. "Angela is telling me one of the poachers is following us. I can't go home now! If I give you the cubs, the poachers will see them and be after you!"

"Okay," Knocker replied softly. "Let's back track just a bit to the hilly area, so we can make a plan. Then we can hide in the hills while looking around to see who might be following us," Knocker added with urgency. "If for any reason I stop and talk with whomever is following us, you must keep going! Keep the cubs with you. If you are holding them, they can't be seen! Angela can lead you to the hills where you will be safe!"

"Can't you just contact Guardian and have him rescue you and the cubs?" Sara asked, looking for some way to keep Knocker and the cubs safe. Her invisibility would not protect them if she let go of the bag.

"No," Knocker whispered. "If the person following us has a gun, he can shoot at me and hit the cubs in the few seconds before we can get away." Knocker looked around quickly, trying to see if he could locate who might be following them. "They may be watching me now. You must hold the cubs, and I will not leave until you and the cubs are safe!"

Sara would not argue further, Knocker had to complete his mission before he could return to his home.

Knocker went quickly ahead but stopped after a few steps and took a several deep breaths. Motioning for Sara to pass him, he stood facing into the woods behind them. Sara went ahead, thinking that Knocker must want to protect her from anyone following them, and that he would follow behind her.

Sara made it up the first slope and looked back, worried because she couldn't hear Knocker's footsteps following her. She could see him standing with his back facing her at the bottom of the slope, he was looking into the darkness behind them.

"Sara," Knocker backed up towards her but did not turn around. "You must continue with the cubs. I will take care of this human following us!" he whispered.

"Are you sure?" Sara asked. "You could hide with me and be safe!"

"No, I don't think this human will leave without some encouragement!" Knocker replied with determination. Taking a deep breath, he continued, "You take the cubs and hide. There are two humans out there now following us. This must be Wayne's group, looking for Doug's cubs."

Knocker stopped to think for a moment, then added, "I need to find out where the third one is—there were three in Wayne's group up by the cave."

"Make sure you stay in touch with Angela, Sara," Knocker said. "She can keep you and the cubs safe. I will find you later!"

"Okay, Knocker, just be careful!" Sara replied as she headed into the dark forest ahead, searching in the moonlight for a place to hide among the hills.

Sara headed into the darkness alone and hid behind a large tree surrounded by shrubs. She knew that her invisibility would hide her from sight, but the sounds of breaking branches and crunching leaves would give away her location. At night, sound was just as useful as sight when tracking your prey, and she and these cubs were their prey!

Putting the bag strap over her shoulder, she held the bag with the cubs close to her chest with one hand, and her other hand reached for her necklace, hoping Angela would keep her calm, so she could protect the cubs.

"Hold on, little buddies, not too much longer now!" She whispered to them.

She heard the soft cries of the little cubs, they were frightened. Sara thought of where Knocker might be, hoping he would be safe. We have the cubs, now we just need to get away!

"Shhh, little ones! You are safe now!" she whispered, trying to comfort them. "We need to wait for Knocker to come back!"

ANOTHER PATH

S ara peered through the leaves into the darkness at the bottom of the hill, trying to see if Knocker was safe. Trees blocked most of her view, but she could hear people running through the forest. Within a few minutes, she could hear some voices yelling, and recognized one as Wayne, the person who had barged into their house earlier this evening.

"Hey, boy, what are you doing out at night?" Wayne shouted out to Knocker as he got closer to him. "You know there's a curfew, right?"

Sara could not hear a response from Knocker, although Wayne must have brought some dogs with him, as she heard a low growling sound, intermixed with the conversation. When the poachers weren't yelling, she was too far away to understand what was being said.

Suddenly, there was shouting coming out of the forest close the Sara, and Wayne reacted immediately.

"What did you say, Blane?" Wayne shouted. "You heard the cubs? Where are you?"

Sara heard a large roar, then footsteps running towards her, along with a lot of shouting from the men.

Angela called out to Sara, conveying an urgent message. "Knocker says to get away with the cubs before you are found, go to Ituria!" Sara remembered Knocker's instructions, if he said to go, she must go immediately! Stepping into an open space where she could see the moon, she shouted, "Guardian, I need help now!" Then she held the bag of cubs close and closed her eyes as she heard footsteps running quickly her way.

Within seconds a blue flash of light hit her just for a second, and then she felt herself being transported to Ituria's Island. Then she lost consciousness.

"Sara, Sara—wake up!" Sara rolled to the right and let go of the bag with the cubs.

"There are the cubs, she must be close!" a voice called, waking Sara from a deep sleep.

"Where are we?" she called out groggily. "Who are you?"

"Sara, you are on the moon, we must get back and rescue Knocker!" The voice called to her, urging her to fully awaken.

Sara sat up with a start. Angela said she was on the moon—right! Guardian would have transported them. She remembered she was invisible—she was protecting the cubs—where are they? Sara looked around anxiously.

"Where are the cubs?" Sara called out, hoping the voice she heard was friendly.

"Sara, I can hear you, but we can't see you," Ituria answered. "We have taken the bag with the cubs and will get them some help; several are very ill. Where is Knocker?"

"He stayed behind, he did not want me to reveal the cubs, so told me to come here—I must go back!" Sara said, panicking when she realized that Knocker was now on his own, with two sets of poachers chasing him.

"Yes, Sara, as soon as you are ready. Here is Knocker's bag, it has the translation stone that will allow you to talk to Knocker. It will become invisible when you hold it to you," Ituria replied in a concerned voice. "Call out to Knocker when you return, and he will find you. He cannot see you, but his sense of smell is extraordinary."

Sara watched as Ituria put the duffle bag down near her, he was looking around, not quite sure where he should leave it. "Sara, you must call to Guardian to transport you, as he will focus on your voice—pick up the bag and call to him, ask him to send you home!"

Sara reached out and picked up the bag, which became invisible in her arms. "Guardian," she called out, "I need to go back to Knocker!"

A column of blue light surrounded Sara, and she felt herself being transported through the beam on her way back to Earth. Try as she might, she could not stay awake during the journey, and was returned to the forest invisible and asleep.

"Sara, you must wake and let Knocker know we have returned!" Sara heard a voice calling out to her as she was sleeping, waking her from her slumber. Angela was reminding her, she needed to let Knocker know she was back!

Quickly looking around, Sara could not see the poachers, so she called out, "Knocker, we are back!"

The roar of an animal in the distance seemed to be answering her call and she sat up to see what was going on. What next? She grasped her necklace in her hand, and whispered, "Angela, what should I do now?"

"Knocker is on his way, stay here!" That's all Sara needed to hear. She would not leave this spot; Angela was receiving messages from Knocker, and Sara would wait until he found her. Ituria said Knocker had a great sense of smell and could find her even if she was invisible; she hoped he was right!

Footsteps running through the forest towards her made Sara crouch to the ground near a large tree. Even though she was invisible, she did not want anyone to trip over her. She would not call out just in case it wasn't Knocker heading in her direction. Turning to the sound of the footsteps, she waited to see who would appear. Voices and the dog growling were getting closer, and Sara could now hear several people running in her direction.

"Wait up, boy!" Wayne shouted. "I'm not done talking with you yet!"

Chapter Sixteen

CONFRONTATION

Appearing first in the opening in front of Sara, Knocker walked quickly over to where she was hiding and urgently whispered to her. "Sara, no matter what you see or hear, do not say anything! Do not let them know you are here!" Knocker then turned to face the men that were following him as they entered the open area.

"How do you know who Doug is, do you work for him?" Wayne yelled at Knocker.

"Nope, just the same way I know your name, Wayne, I listen." Knocker said calmly. "So, if you want to rescue the cubs, you should head north, okay? I saw they had a truck a little bit up the road. That may be how they are going to take the cubs over the border."

"Have you seen the cubs?" Wayne asked warily as he stepped closer to Knocker. "How many are there?"

"No, I didn't see them. Not sure where they would be right now," Knocker replied, not moving as Wayne approached. "Doug might have them in a cage or something."

"Why should I believe you?" Wayne's voice changed to a threatening tone. "Why don't you just come with me and show me where you saw Doug's group, okay?"

"I don't think so," Knocker replied calmly. "You have permission to be in these woods at night, remember? Apparently, I don't, so I don't want you to be reporting me to anyone."

"At this point, you don't have a choice, boy!" Wayne said in a menacing voice. "You will accompany me and show me where those cubs are, or I will turn you in to the authorities!"

"You may want to reconsider your demands, as I am not going to accompany you or help you capture the cubs." Knocker replied, his voice steady, no hint of emotion.

Sara held her breath, trying not to move as Knocker stood his ground against Wayne; what would Knocker do next? She held her necklace tight in her hand, hoping Angela's spirit would calm her. "Do not worry Sara, Knocker will protect you!"

"Look boy," Wayne argued as he glared at Knocker. "There are three of us and only one of you! You will show us where the cubs are!"

Knocker responded confidently; showing he was not scared by Wayne's threats. "I know you are not here to rescue these cubs as you said before. I know you are here to steal them and sell them across the border."

Wayne anger got the better of him. "Listen, what I do with the cubs is none of your business! You just need to show me where they are, got it?!"

"No, this has gone on long enough!" Knocker's green eyes were glowing, staring directly at Wayne as he continued, his voice low and calculated. "I will give you one chance to leave this forest now, or I will make it so you will never leave!"

The two other men came over and stood beside Wayne, ready to protect him from this teenager and whatever he might be planning.

"Look," Wayne started, trying to sound friendly, "we just want the cubs, that's all. Then we'll let you go home, okay?"

"No! That is not okay!" Knocker's voice was defiant now, and his fists were clenched. "Your options are to leave, or to remain forever in this forest! What is your choice?"

Sara could tell Knocker was furious at this point; but didn't know what he could do against these three men.

Wayne looked at the other two men, nodded to them and waved his hand to have them circle around Knocker. They split up and started moving slowly around, one on each side of Knocker.

Knocker took a step back, and remarked with surprising calmness, "Is it your choice to remain in this forest forever?" That made them stop in their tracks, looking at each other and then at Wayne, trying to figure out what Knocker meant.

Shaking his fist at Knocker, Wayne stated, "Look, this is how we make our money, and some boy has no right to interfere, got it?"

Knocker's reaction was immediate, and Sara watched in awe as this teenage boy transformed into a gigantic dragon, his wings reaching high into the trees and green eyes glowing, staring ominously at Wayne. Before the men could react, Knocker grabbed their rifles in his dragon jaws and chomped on them, breaking them into several pieces, scattering as they fell to the ground.

"What if a dragon decides to interfere with you?" Knocker shouted.

Frozen in place with their mouths open and eyes wide, they stared at the dragon in front of them and then at their rifles broken into pieces on the ground. They were too afraid to move, still in total disbelief.

"You will leave now," Knocker commanded them. "And if I find you in this forest again, you will have to answer to me, and I do not give second chances—do you understand?"

Wayne was the first to react, shouting quickly as he turned to run, "We're gone, you won't see us again! Come on guys!" He started running towards the road, the other two following close behind.

Knocker watched the men as they disappeared in the forest towards the road, then crouched down and whispered to where Sara was hiding. "Sara, give me a few moments to return to human form, it requires a lot of concentration."

Sara watched in silence as Knocker took several minutes to transform from a ferocious dragon back to the form of a teenage boy. "Knocker, are you okay?" she whispered.

"Yes, Sara," he replied calmly. "I try not to reveal my true form, but I could think of no other way to get those poachers to leave the forest. Now we must get you home, in case they head that way, okay?"

Chapter Seventeen

RACE FOR HOME

"**S**ara," Knocker whispered quietly, "we need to get you home before you are missed. I cannot see you, but I can smell you are near. If you follow me, I will lead you back to your home."

"Okay, Knocker," she replied. "I agree we need to get home before my father misses me. Hopefully, all the poachers are gone now, and I can sneak into my room. How long does the invisibility potion last?"

Knocker answered, "It usually lasts three to four hours, depending on the human's metabolism. It has been almost three hours so far, so you will need to remain hidden until you are visible. Let's go, follow me!" Knocker continued as he turned and headed towards Sara's house.

Sara followed Knocker in the dark, keeping close so she wouldn't get lost. While she had difficulty seeing with only the moonlight, he seemed to be comfortable walking in the dark and moved quickly through the trees. As they got close to her home, he slowed down, and motioned for Sara to stop.

"Sara," he said as he turned in her direction, "there seems to be a disturbance at your home. The first group of poachers is outside."

"What?" Sara exclaimed. "Why would they be there?"

"Listen to me," Knocker replied. "You can get into your house, you are invisible. Go directly to your room and hide. Block the door, do whatever is needed so that no one sees you until you are visible again. Okay?"

Holding her necklace tight, she knew she had to be back inside before they missed her. "Okay, Knocker! You stay safe, they can't see me, so I'll run into the house!"

"Angela will keep me advised of your status, and I will help if needed, but it is best if we can keep your activities tonight a secret, if I get involved it may cause complications," Knocker responded. "Now, go! Hurry!"

"I'm going!" Sara responded quickly as she went past Knocker towards her house.

Doug was standing at the front door, so Sara focused on getting to the back door that she had left unlocked. She passed quietly by two of the poachers standing in the road, and she could hear the third banging on the door.

"Open this door!" Doug shouted.

"What is the matter?" Sara's father yelled back, not wanting to open the door. "Someone already checked this house tonight. Me and my children have not left."

"Who came last time?" was the reply.

"I don't know his name, he said he had to check to all houses, and he came in and woke me, my son and daughter up to confirm we were home!" he responded.

"Look, I don't know who it was last time, but he wasn't supposed to be here. Now let me in!" Doug was coming into the house, whether Sara's father let him in or not!

Running quickly to the back of the house, Sara went in the back door and bolted it from the inside. Then she snuck into her room and closed the door. She locked the door and put a chair under the door handle, so it would not open. She was still invisible!

"Let me in now!" Doug demanded once again.

"Okay, let me get the lock!" her father replied, and she could hear him fumbling with the door lock, to get it open.

"Now, get everyone who lives here out into the living room," Doug yelled.

"Samuel and Sara!" her father called nervously. "Please come out and let this man know you are here!"

Walking slowly out of his room, Samuel walked over to his father, standing next to him, and asked, "What's going on father? Didn't they already check us tonight?"

"Yes, but this is someone else," his father replied. "I don't know who the other guy was, maybe he was a poacher."

"Did he tell you his name, boy?" Doug asked in a threatening tone.

"No, he just made me come out here, and then told me to go back to bed," Samuel answered quietly. "He said he was with the authorities."

"Okay," Doug said. "Is there anyone else here?"

"Yes," replied Sara's father, "my daughter, Sara."

"Well, get her out here! I need to know who is in this house, and I need to know now!" Doug yelled at him.

"Sara, I need you to come out of your room for a minute," her father said. "The authorities want to make sure everyone is here!"

Sara looked at where her hands would be, she was still invisible! She can't go out now!

"Father, I'm frightened!" she yelled through the door. "Please make them go away!"

Sara pulled her blanket off her bed to see if it would cover her, but when she wrapped it around herself, she noticed that portions of it became invisible too. That won't work!

"Who is that?" Doug demanded.

"That is my daughter," Sara's father answered. "The last guy who came here was very mean and she was frightened. Please, don't make her go through this again."

"Is she the only one in there?" Doug yelled. "Where is her mother?"

"Her mother, my wife, died several years ago," Sara's father said sadly. "It is only me and my two children now."

Doug walked over to the door and jiggled the handle, but the door did not open. Sara slipped under the bed, not knowing if he would break the door in or not.

"Father," she called out again. "Please make them go away!"

Chapter Eighteen

New Member of the Alliance

"Look," her father argued to Doug. "You know she's in there, you can hear her. She's just a little girl and you are scaring her. What else do you need?"

"Okay—I'll let it go this time!" Doug snarled at him. "But if I have to come back here again, I'm going to bust that door down. You make sure you and your family don't go out at night, do you understand?"

"We understand," he replied slowly, hoping Doug would just go away and leave his family alone. "We will not go out at night."

Doug stomped out of the house and slammed the front door, still mad the tiger cubs he wanted to sell had disappeared. Sara could hear him yell to his group as he left. "Tony, grab Randy and tell him we're going to find Wayne and get those cubs back!"

Sara breathed a sigh of relief, but she did not come out from under the bed. She couldn't let her father in either, not until she was visible.

"Knocker will wait outside until all is clear." Sara was glad Angela was in touch with Knocker, but she was worried for his safety. What if Doug saw him outside her house? She hoped that he was far enough away so he wouldn't be found. Now, she just had to wait until she became visible again.

A soft knock on the door was followed by her father calling to her, "Sara, are you okay now? That man is gone."

"Father," Sara replied anxiously. "Thank you for keeping him from coming into my room or making me come out! I'm still very frightened and want to leave the door locked, just in case he comes back, okay?" She hoped her father wouldn't try and come in.

"Are you sure, Sara?" he asked. "You are safe now, he has gone. There is only me and Samuel in the house now."

"Yes, I will be okay, but I'm just so upset now—I will try to calm down and go to sleep, but I want to keep the door locked, okay? Just to make sure. I don't think I can go to sleep otherwise." Sara's voice was very anxious, but it wasn't so much about Doug, but that her father should come into the room, and she was not yet visible.

"Okay, Sara," her father replied. "Please try to get some sleep! We will be leaving early in the morning, and you must stay in the house tomorrow. Something must be going on outside since we have had two of these guys come into the house."

"Yes, father," Sara agreed. "I promise I won't go out of the house tomorrow. Please keep yourself and Samuel safe! Good night and thank you for keeping that man out of my room!"

"You stay there where you feel safe," he answered sympathetically. "I will make sure Samuel and I are safe at the logging site, and I'll let you know when we are leaving in the morning so you can bolt the front door from the inside. Then, if you want to stay in your room until we get back, that is fine!"

"Thank you!" Sara said with relief. "Thank you for keeping him out! I will be better in the morning, I promise!"

Waiting under the bed, it was Angela who let her know that the invisibility spell had worn off about half an hour later. "Sara, you are visible again. Knocker is still outside waiting to confirm your safety." Sara crawled out from under the bed, relieved that she could see her arms and legs, she was visible again! She quietly unlocked the bedroom door and then opened the back door where Knocker was waiting.

Stepping out to the backyard, she whispered, "Knocker, are you okay? I'm fine so you can return home now!"

"Hi Sara," Knocker replied softly as he stepped out from the shadows. "Glad to see you are safe!"

"Thank you for rescuing the cubs, Knocker," Sara said. "Please, if you are ever in the area again and need my help, I will be glad to help on your missions to rescue the animals in this area from the poachers!"

"Thank you, Sara, for your courage and bravery tonight, as well as your offer to help in the future," Knocker answered. "Because of your special relationship with Angela and your knowledge of the area, we may need to ask for your assistance again, as these poachers do not show any sign of stopping their killing and stealing of the tigers and their cubs."

"I am glad to do whatever I can to protect these animals," Sara replied with determination in her voice. "They need someone to watch out for them, and Angela and I will do our best to help keep them safe."

"We will need to keep our activities secret, Sara, as the poachers have direct ties to the government, and could be very dangerous for you and your family if they learn you may be involved," Knocker explained. "We do have several humans that are part of Ituria's Alliance, and I am glad to add you to that group!"

"Now," he continued, "as you have noted, I need to return home. Please be safe and take care of yourself and your family. And remember, you are courageous and brave, as you have proven several times tonight. Welcome to Ituria's Alliance!" Knocker bowed to Sara, then stepped back into the darkness. "Farewell and be safe!"

"Take care, Knocker," Sara replied, then moved back into the doorway. "I look forward to meeting you again soon. You can call to Angela, as she can hear you and will relay to me when you are here."

Staying in the doorway until she saw the blue flash of light signaling Knocker had returned to the moon, she then closed the door and bolted it. As she silently walked back to her room, Sara held her necklace and thought about the secret missions to come. She was glad that she and Angela could do something to help protect the local animals, especially the beautiful tigers! She was proud to be a new member of Ituria's Alliance!

THE END
—until Sara's next secret mission!

NOTE FROM THE AUTHOR

Although this is a fantasy adventure, the dangers to the Amur Tiger (also known as Siberian Tiger) are very real. Poachers hunt them for sport or to sell their bodies to other countries for "medicine." The increased logging into primeval forests has given humans greater access to "accidently" run into a tiger and illegally shoot it. Hunting for tigers was outlawed over 75 years ago when the number of wild tigers in the Amur Tiger territory dropped to as few as 30 tigers. A recent count had it close to 600, however, outlawing the hunting of tigers only stopped the law-abiding citizens. Poachers don't care about laws, as they bribe local government officials to look the other way as they transport their cargo.

The current government says they are protecting these beautiful tigers and only 10 to 15 tigers were poached in 2020. However, it has been estimated that between 50-70 tigers were killed in 2020 and a similar number in 2021 in the protected areas. These totals were based on sales data collected from the illegal tiger-parts buyers, and they far exceed the reported number by the official government spokesman.

Hunting by poachers is not the only danger these beautiful creatures must overcome. Illegal logging and deforestation where they reside takes away their source of food. As predators, tigers rely on local animals to survive; however, the wild boars and deer no longer have the forest to protect them nor its bounty to supply them food, so they must move or starve.

Until the government actively enforces its laws against hunting these tigers, as well as stop the illegal logging that gives poachers access to their homes, there is no safety for them. They are killed "for sport" whenever they are found, or actively hunted to sell illegally across borders. Let's hope that something changes soon, before these wonderful creatures are just ghosts from the past.

National Geographic Article – *Siberian tigers are being hunted at night for their body parts,* by Dina Fine Maron – published January 19, 2022

National Geographic Article – *From Trees to Tigers, Case Shows Cost of Illegal Logging* – by Jani Hall – Published November 10, 2015

World Wildlife Fund Review 2013 – *Illegal logging in the Russian Far East: Global Demand and Taiga Destruction* – Smirnov, D.Y. (ed.) Kabanets, A.G., Milakovsky, B.J., Lepeshkin, E.A., Sychikov, D.V. 2013 WWF, Moscow

Book Club Questions

1. What caused Sara to leave her house in the middle of the night?
2. Where did Sara get her necklace?
3. What happens when Sara holds her necklace in her hand?
4. Who is Angela?
5. What did Wayne's group mean when they said they were going to acquire Doug's cubs?
6. Why couldn't Sara let her father into her room after she finished her mission with Knocker?
7. Why is it important to enforce laws prohibiting illegal poaching and illegal lumber harvesting?
8. What happens when you cut down entire forests? What is lost besides the trees themselves?
9. How does the existence of a primeval (old growth) forest effect humans outside of the forest?
10. Something to think about—why is it important to preserve primeval (old growth) forests and their native inhabitants?

About the Author

J.B. moved to Florida in her early teens and has lived there ever since, enjoying the mild weather and abundance of wildlife. She even spent several seasons raising orphan squirrels. She graduated from the University of Central Florida and has spent her working career in the legal profession. Her novels are inspired by her family and nature, as well as her need to escape from the real world once in a while.

www.facebook.com/J.B.Moonstar
Instagram@J.B.Moonstar
Twitter@jb_moonstar
Jbmoonstar.author@gmail.com
Website – jbmoonstar.com

DISCOVER MORE BY
JB MOONSTAR

CHRONICLES OF ITURIA
Russ and The Hidden Voice
Taylor and the Red Wolf Rescue
Jenna and the Legend of the White Wolf
Jenna and the Eyes of Fire
Jan and the Secret Cave
Jan and the Search for Lilya
Taylor and the Final Nine
Michelle and the Missing Manatee
Jenna and the Broken Promise
Sara and the Secret Mission
& More Adventures to Come!

THE MERMAIDS OF CRYSTAL CAY
Kimmi and the Sea Dragon
Roselia and the Ancient Warriors
& More Adventures to Come!

COLORING BOOK FROM
ARTIST JENN KOTICK
Mermaids

Discover more at
4HorsemenPublications.com

10% off using HORSEMEN10

www.ingramcontent.com/pod-product-compliance
Lightning Source LLC
Chambersburg PA
CBHW031547310726
48971CB00008B/2661